When You Are Camping

Anne Lee

Kane Miller
A DIVISION OF EDC PUBLISHING

First Edition
Kane Miller, A Division of EDC Publishing

Text and illustrations copyright © Anne Lee 2012

Library of Congress Control Number: 2011924320

Manufactured by Regent Publishing Services, Hong Kong
Printed September 2011 in ShenZhen, Guangdong, China

ISBN: 978-1-61067-064-7

1 2 3 4 5 6 7 8 9 10

To Greta and Tallulah, my two girls who love camping, and to Ginnie and Glenn, who keep Big Bend the best place to camp.

Hazel and Tilly wake up, and it is raining. It is raining hard – on the tent, on the camp chairs, on the tarp over the picnic table. The rain makes a crackling noise on the tent, and Dad gets wet making hot chocolate.

Tilly likes camping. You can eat marshmallows for breakfast when you are camping.

Tilly and Hazel put on their raincoats.
It rains and rains, and they splash in puddles.

They run through wet grass. They run down a path in the woods.

Tilly sees a green frog who has come out to splash too.

Hazel likes camping. You can get really muddy when you are camping.

The rain stops, and Tilly watches a caterpillar climb up the tall grass. It takes a long time, but Tilly doesn't mind waiting.

Hazel can't wait. She chases white moths around the tent and sneaks up on a gray rabbit very, very slowly... But not slowly enough.

Tilly watches and watches her caterpillar. Tilly likes camping. You can make a new friend when you are camping.

Mom helps Hazel and Tilly put on their bathing suits. Dad blows up two yellow tubes, and they go to the river.

Minnows dart around their ankles and toes.
Tilly floats on her tube and watches for fat fish swimming in the water.

Hazel takes her tube spinning and splashing through the current. Hazel likes camping.

You can take a bath with fish when you are camping.

After dinner everybody goes for a walk.

The sun is hanging low behind the mountains,
and the woods begin to feel dark.

Tilly sees a deer standing very still, listening.

Hazel sees it too, and then they watch the deer run away through the trees.
Hazel and Tilly like camping.

You can see a million fireflies when you are camping.

Dad makes popcorn, and Mom tells a story by the campfire.

It is time for bed. Tilly climbs into her green sleeping bag.
Hazel climbs into her blue sleeping bag. Dad turns on the lantern.

Hazel loves camping. Tilly loves camping.
Crickets sing you to sleep when you are camping.

Anne Lee was raised in Colorado, and currently lives in Pittsburgh,
Pennsylvania. She is an artist, illustrator, and children's librarian.
She has been camping since she was two years old, and happily
camps today with her husband, daughters, and adventurous friends.
You can view Anne's online gallery at www.anneleestudio.com.

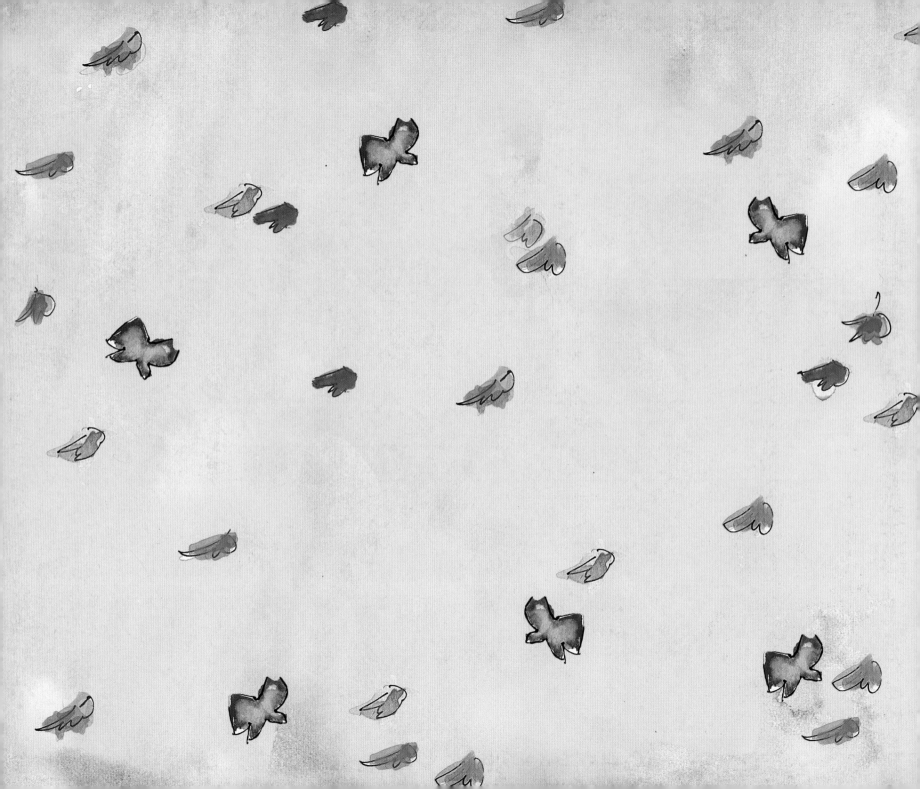